This book belongs to

_____

_____

_____

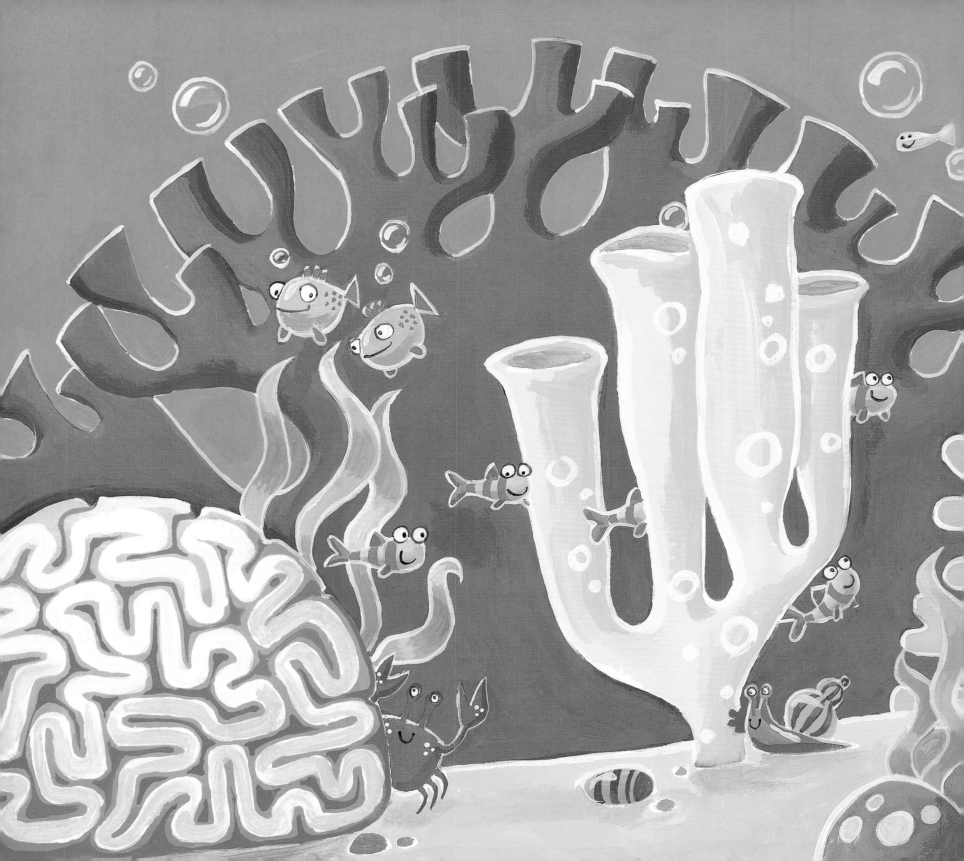

To Wayne, with love

tiger tales
an imprint of ME Media, LLC
202 Old Ridgefield Road, Wilton, CT 06897
This paperback edition published 2005
Published in hardcover in the United States 2003
Originally published in Great Britain 2003
By Little Tiger Press
An imprint of Magi Publications
Text and illustrations copyright © 2003 Ruth Galloway
ISBN-10: 1-58925-391-4
ISBN-13: 978-1-58925-391-9
Printed in the United States of America

Library of Congress Cataloging-in-Publication Data
Galloway, Ruth, 1973–
  Smiley Shark / by Ruth Galloway.
    p. cm.
Summary: Smiley Shark's toothy smile frightens the other sea animals but
comes in handy when they are caught in a net.
  ISBN 1-58925-028-1 (Hardcover)
  ISBN 1-58925-391-4 (Paperback)
  [1. Sharks—Fiction. 2. Smile—Fiction. 3. Marine animals—Fiction.]
I. Title.
  PZ7.G3853 Sm 2003
  [E]—dc21
                                          2002014261

Smiley Shark

by Ruth Galloway

tiger tales

Far away, in a deep rolling ocean, lived Smiley Shark—
the smiliest and sunniest, the friendliest and funniest,
the biggest and toothiest of all the fish.

Every day Smiley Shark watched the beautiful fish that dipped and dived, jiggled and jived, and darted and dashed with a splish and a splash.

Smiley Shark longed to splish and splash
with the other fish. But whenever he
smiled at them they swam away.

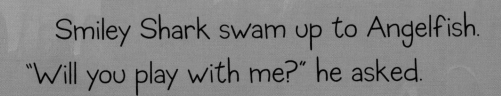

Smiley Shark swam up to Angelfish.
"Will you play with me?" he asked.

Angelfish shivered and shook, then . . .

SWOOSH!

She raced
away as fast
as she could.

Puffer was blowing bubbles.

"That looks fun!" laughed Smiley Shark.

But Puffer blew himself up into a big spiky

ball and pricked poor Smiley Shark on the nose!

Starfish was twirling and whirling,
dancing and prancing.
"What fun!" giggled Smiley Shark.
But . . .

SWIRL!

Starfish
twirled off
across the ocean floor.

Smiley Shark showed his
toothy smile to Jellyfish . . .

and Octopus . . .

and Catfish.

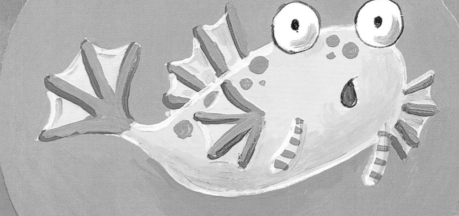

In a flash, they all took off
as fast as they could swim.

"Everyone is scared of my big white teeth," wailed Smiley Shark. He didn't feel much like smiling anymore.

SPLISH! SPLASH!

Twisting and turning, splashing and churning,
the fish danced faster than ever. Smiley Shark
watched from a distance. But this time something
was very wrong. All the fish were . . .

TRAPPED!

"Help!" cried the fish. "Please help us, Smiley Shark!"

Smiley Shark swam around and around the fisherman's net.

What could he do? How could he help? The only thing Smiley Shark could do was . . .

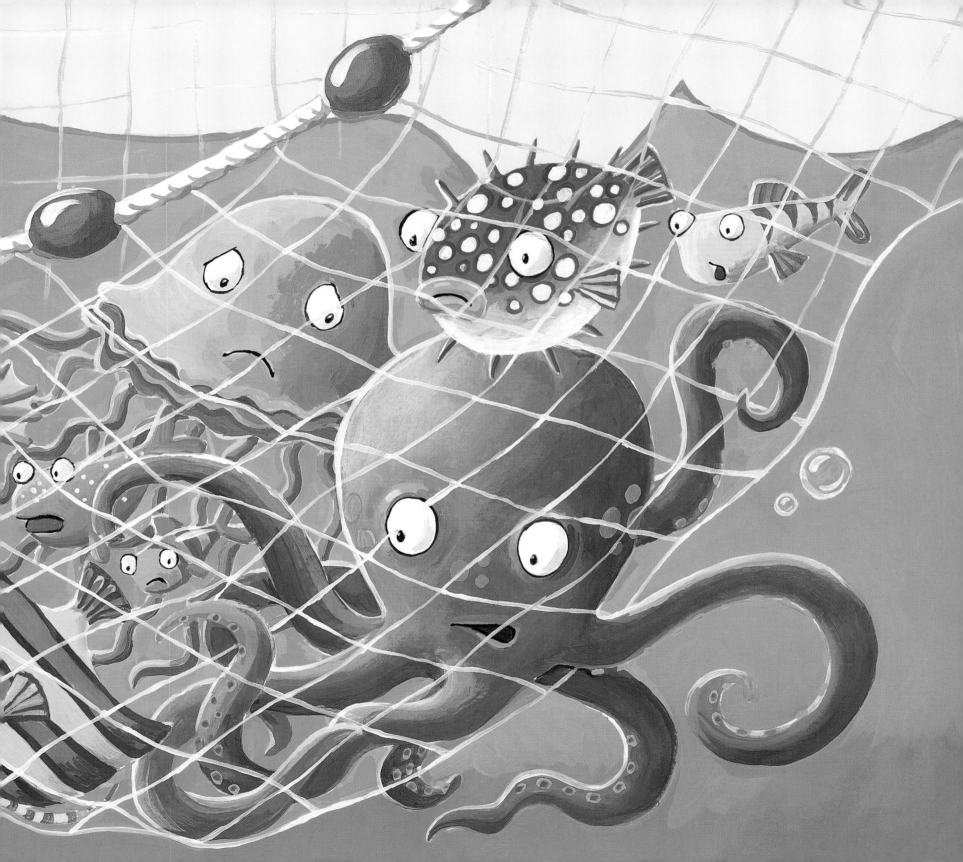

SMILE!

"Aaaaaaaahhhh!" screamed the fisherman, dropping his heavy net into the waves. "I'm getting out of here!" he cried.

"Hurray!" cheered the fish. "We're safe!
Thank you, Smiley Shark!"

Now, far away in the deep rolling ocean,
live Smiley Shark and all his friends!
And every day they can be seen,
dipping and diving, darting and
dashing, splishing and
splashing and . . .

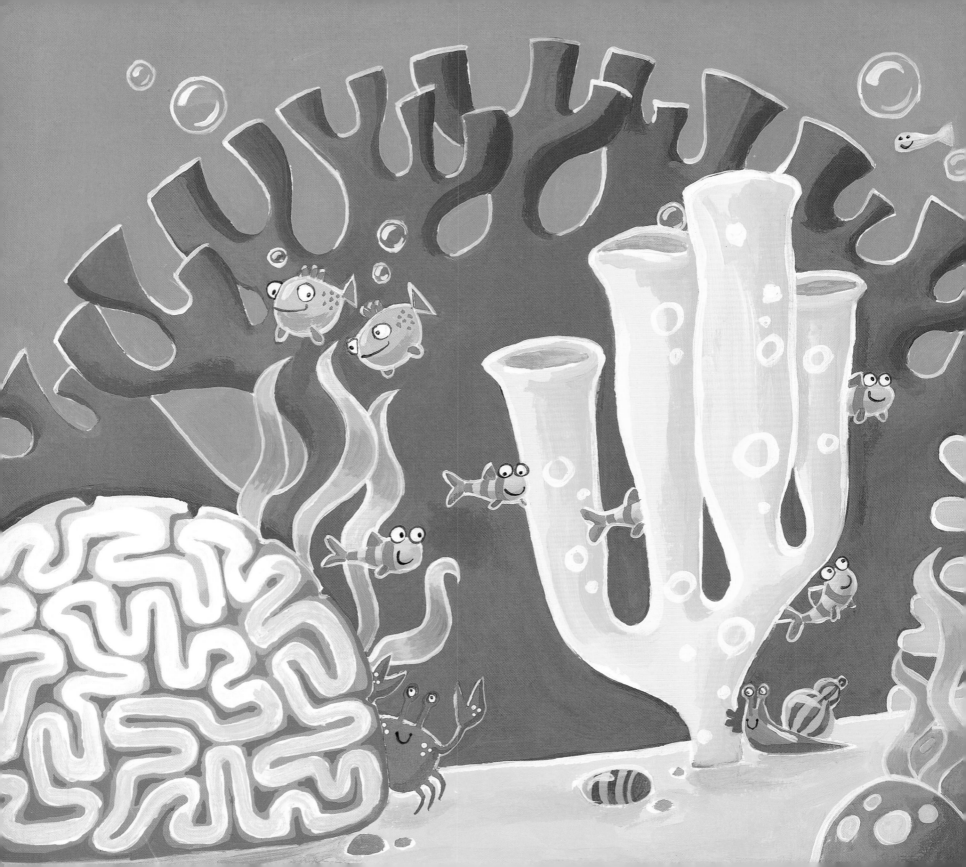

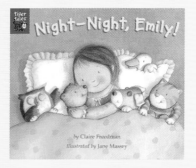

Night-Night, Emily!
by Claire Freedman
illustrated by Jane Massey
ISBN 1-58925-390-6

Where There's a Bear, There's Trouble!
by Michael Catchpool
illustrated by Vanessa Cabban
ISBN 1-58925-389-2

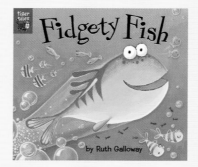

Fidgety Fish
by Ruth Galloway
ISBN 1-58925-377-9

Snarlyhissopus
by Alan MacDonald
illustrated by Louise Voce
ISBN 1-58925-370-1

Explore the world of tiger tales!

More fun-filled and exciting stories await you!
Look for these titles and more at your local library or bookstore.
And have fun reading!

tiger tales

202 Old Ridgefield Road, Wilton, CT 06897

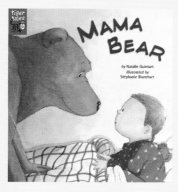

Mama Bear
by Natalie Quintart
illustrated by Stéphanie Blanchart
ISBN 1-58925-394-9

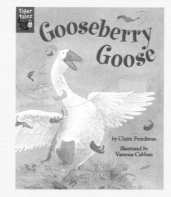

Gooseberry Goose
by Claire Freedman
illustrated by Vanessa Cabban
ISBN 1-58925-392-2

**The Von Hamm Family:
Alex and the Tart**
by Guido van Genechten
ISBN 1-58925-393-0

Louie and the Monsters
by Ella Burfoot
ISBN 1-58925-395-7